ANONYMOUS

Blood, Ink, And Concrete

To the misfits and the rebels,
The ones who never fit the mold,
Who dance in the shadows,
And laugh in the face of conformity.

To those who wear their scars as badges,
And turn their pain into power,
Who blaze their own trails,
And light fires where others see only darkness.

This one's for the warriors of the unseen,
The dreamers who dare to defy,
Who rise from the ashes,
And forge their path through the storm.

For you, the restless spirits,
Who challenge the world and shape it,

"Ink bleeds into the concrete, and our stories are etched in stone."

Anonymous

Contents

Foreword

Welcome to the edge of your comfort zone, where the rules are bent and the lines are blurred. You're about to dive into a world where shadows have their own stories and the noise is louder than the silence. This isn't just a book; it's a journey through the grit and grind of a reality that's raw and unapologetic.

We're not here to sugarcoat the truth or polish the pain. We're here to confront it head-on, to face the chaos and the contradictions that shape our world. This is a space where every word is a rebellion, every page a battleground for the truths we've buried.

In these pages, you'll meet the voices of the lost and the damned, the dreamers and the disenchanted. They're not looking for redemption or salvation—they're embracing the messiness of existence, turning their struggles into their strength. The poetry here isn't meant to comfort; it's meant to challenge, to provoke, to spark something deep within you.

This is where we strip away the pretense and get real. We dig into the darkness, unearth the raw edges, and let the unfiltered emotions bleed through. It's a sonic explosion of words that'll make you question, reflect, and maybe even rebel.

So, if you're ready to push past the superficial and dive into the heart of the storm, keep reading. This is where the real fight begins, where the echoes of our struggles transform into anthems of defiance.

Welcome to the noise. Welcome to the chaos. Welcome to the truth.

Acknowledgments

Cover shot courtesy of Evgeniy Grozev, captured from Pexels.com.

Concrete Jungle Dreams

Concrete beats where the thunder don't sleep,
   Steel heart thumps to the pulse of the street.
   A city that grinds but never gets neat,
   Hungry mouths chasing a life they can't eat.

Dreams wrapped in the grime of the hustle,
   Muscle and sweat, the pain and the tussle.
   Flash of the lights, man, it's just a rustle,
   Lost in the noise, drowning in struggle.

Crumbling blocks where hope's a facade,
   Echoes of shots in the veins of the squad.
   Chase what you crave, but it's always a fraud,
   A ghost in the smoke, a wink from the god.

City built on the bones of the lost,
   Dreams sell cheap, but they come with a cost.
   Broken down doors, broken down trust,
   Promises cracked, left choking on dust.

Climbing the ladder where rungs don't exist,
   Concrete jungle, where nothing is blissed.

But we grind, still we grind, with that clenched fist,
Eyes on the prize, though the shadows twist.

Concrete jungle, where dreams never sleep,
Blood in the gutter, and secrets to keep.
Rise or fall, in the depths we creep,
Concrete jungle, where the weak can't leap.

Ink, Blood, and Betrayal

Ink in the veins, flowing like lies,
  Blood in the streets, where the truth dies.
  Words on the wall, painted in cries,
  Trust breaks sharp, like shattered ties.

We carved our names in the concrete slate,
  Bond thick as thieves, but the knife came late.
  Loyalty pledged, but it couldn't hold weight,
  In the dark, whispers twist, changing fate.

Handshakes cold, like the night's last breath,
  Promises deep, now they echo with death.
  Streetlights flicker, showing signs of regret,
  The ink runs dry, but the scars stay wet.

Blood on the hands, but it's not my own,
  Betrayal's kiss, like a crack in the stone.
  Eyes once bright, now hard like bone,
  In the mirror, see the faces disowned.

We were brothers, cutting through the noise,
  Raised by the streets, but we weren't boys.

Now trust is a blade that betrays the joys,
Ink spills black, on the paper it toys.

The streets don't care for the bond you break,
Friendship's a game, and the price you stake.
Ink, blood, betrayal—all that's at stake,
And in the end, it's your soul they take.

Ink in the veins, but it dries to dust,
Blood in the streets, where the echoes rust.
Once was trust, now it's just disgust,
Ink, blood, betrayal—where's the justice in lust?

Rebel Heart

I walk the line, but I don't fit the frame,
  Break the mold, I'm rejecting the shame.
  Society's chains, man, they're all the same,
  But I'm carving my path, redefining the game.

Voices scream, but I'm deaf to the crowd,
  Drown in their noise, but I'm standing proud.
  I'm not here to blend, I'm here to be loud,
  Rebel heart beats, no heads in the cloud.

They say conform, but I shatter the rule,
  Not a puppet, I ain't nobody's fool.
  I rise, I fall, but I won't be your tool,
  My fire burns hot, like a loaded fuel.

Critics glare, they can't see what I see,
  They're trapped in a box, but I'm running free.
  I fight for the dream, not their reality,
  Rebel heart pumps to its own decree.

Clawing through the dirt, but I don't seek their gold,
  Silver tongues speak, but their words are cold.

I'm a storm in the night, breaking through the fold,
Rebel heart roars, like it's never been told.

I've tasted the scars, but I don't fade away,
Built from the pain, now I light the way.
They want me to break, but I'm here to stay,
Rebel heart lives, and it won't obey.

Bridge the gap between what they want and who I am,
Pushing through the walls, I don't give a damn.
I'm a force, I'm a quake, I'm the final slam,
Rebel heart stands, like a one-man jam.

This is my voice, this is my fight,
In a world so wrong, I'm the one that's right.
I'll burn it down just to see the light,
Rebel heart beats through the endless night.

Lost in the Noise

I'm lost in the noise, can't hear my own sound,
  Drowning in the static, everything's wound.
  Voices collide, but none of them pound,
  Echoes in my head, man, they're spinning me round.

Screens flash bright, but the colors all fade,
  Trapped in the hype, but the truth's a charade.
  I'm stuck in the loop, like a glitch in the grade,
  Chasing the signal, but it's all just a trade.

Caught in the stream, but I'm sinking deep,
  Mind's on overload, I can't even sleep.
  Lost in the data, can't find what I keep,
  Climbing these walls, but the angles are steep.

Information bleeds, but the meaning's gone,
  Everyone's screaming, but it's all a con.
  I'm just trying to breathe, while they pile on,
  Lost in the noise, can't find the dawn.

Thoughts clash hard, like a war in my brain,
  Waves of confusion, pouring like rain.

I reach for the light, but I'm gripped by the pain,
Lost in the noise, feeling the strain.

They say speak up, but my voice gets drowned,
In a sea of opinions, I can't hear the ground.
Searching for truth, but it's nowhere around,
Lost in the noise, it's a deafening sound.

I'm wired in tight, but I'm coming undone,
Trying to stand tall, but the weight's a ton.
Noise in my head, like a loaded gun,
Lost in the noise, where's the quiet gone?

I scream in the dark, but it echoes back,
I run through the maze, but I'm off the track.
Searching for peace in the world's loud attack,
Lost in the noise, trying to find what I lack.

I'm breaking the chains, but they're pulling me down,
Drowning in the voices that wear the crown.
But I'm digging through the noise, finding my own sound,
Lost in the noise, till I turn it around.

Scarred Souls

In the shadows where the past still crawls,
Scarred souls wander through the crumbling halls.
Life's a battlefield, where the pride falls,
Echoes of the hurt, man, the pain calls.

Broken dreams litter the fractured ground,
Silent screams in the night, no one's around.
Heartbeats sync to a desolate sound,
Scarred souls searching, but they're tightly bound.

Ink on my skin, but it's not a design,
It's the trace of the battles, the truth intertwined.
Every mark tells a story, every line's a sign,
Of a life bruised and battered, but it won't resign.

Voices in my head like a constant drone,
Chained to the echoes, where the dark has grown.
Truth's a mirror cracked, every shard overblown,
Scarred souls still fighting, but they're feeling alone.

In the war of the mind, there's no place for rest,
Memories like daggers, tearing through the chest.

Lost in the struggle, can't seem to forget,
Scarred souls waging battles they didn't request.

Shattered hope like glass underfoot,
Each step cuts deep, every wound's absolute.
Still, we walk on through the bitter dispute,
Scarred souls hardened, but never absolute.

City lights flicker, but they blur and fade,
Truth in the chaos, where the fears invade.
We wear the scars like a badge of the frayed,
Scarred souls rising, in the shadows we're made.

Tears mix with blood on this relentless ride,
Wounds from the world, they're buried inside.
But in the darkness, we still strive,
Scarred souls igniting, trying to survive.

Fallen but fighting, we're carving our own,
Through the scars and the pain, where the seeds are sown.
In the heart of the storm, we find our tone,
Scarred souls standing, in a world overthrown.

Street Symphony

Concrete drums beat, in the veins of the city,
   Rhythm in the gutter, but it ain't always pretty.
   Graffiti bass lines, with a pulse that's gritty,
   Street symphony plays, but it's raw and witty.

Neon lights flash, in sync with the grind,
   Each corner's a note, in the chaos we find.
   Siren screams clash with the bassline's bind,
   Urban heartbeat, it's a sound unrefined.

Boots on the pavement, stepping to the beat,
   In the rhythm of the struggle, where the past and future meet.
   Subway echoes rumble, feel the heat in the street,
   Street symphony's alive, in the soles of our feet.

Curbside harmonies with the clash of the horns,
   Broken melodies born where the soul's torn.
   Every alleyway's chorus, where the edge is worn,
   Street symphony's a tale, from the chaos we're sworn.

Graffiti scripts, like verses of the night,
   Streetlights flicker, casting shadows in flight.

Life's a loud crescendo, in the neon light,
Street symphony's a jam, till the morning's first sight.

Skyscrapers hum, like a distant refrain,
Rivers of asphalt, flowing with pain.
In the symphony of the street, nothing's in vain,
Every crash and thud, it's a lyrical chain.

Voices in the wind, like a choir of the lost,
Screaming for redemption, no matter the cost.
Street symphony plays, through the tempest tossed,
In the rhythm of the city, where the lines are crossed.

Turn up the volume, let the heartbeat explode,
In the noise of the street, where the stories are told.
A cacophony of life, with the city as gold,
Street symphony's our anthem, let the truth unfold.

Dance to the sirens, let the beats be our guide,
In the urban symphony, where the dreams collide.
From the grit to the glory, in the heart we reside,
Street symphony's the anthem, and it's amplified.

Toxic Love

We're tangled in a mess, a deadly embrace,
    Hearts bound in chains, but it's all a disgrace.
    Love's a poison, runs deep, no saving grace,
    Toxic love's a mirror, but it's a dark place.

Your eyes are fire, but they scorch and burn,
    Twisted affections, a lesson unlearned.
    Every touch's a thrill, but it's raw and churned,
    Toxic love's a game where the pain's confirmed.

Breath on my neck, but it's stifling tight,
    Caught in the shadows, can't find the light.
    Whispers of poison in the dead of night,
    Toxic love's a storm, and it's ready to fight.

Embers of a flame that'll never die,
    We're burning down bridges, and I don't know why.
    Your voice's a drug, I'm hooked on the high,
    Toxic love's a trap where we both lie.

Chasing the chaos, addicted to pain,
    We're trapped in the storm, drenched in the rain.

Each kiss is a blade, cuts through the chain,
Toxic love's a curse, and it's driving me insane.

We dance in the dark, where the shadows play,
Hearts heavy with the weight of the fray.
A cycle of pain, but we choose to stay,
Toxic love's the drug, and it's leading us astray.

Screams in the silence, echoes in the void,
Love's a battlefield, and we're both destroyed.
Bound in the wreckage, our souls are toyed,
Toxic love's a wound that's never fully healed.

Hollow promises that we can't erase,
Twisted affections, leaving no space.
In the mirror of madness, we see our face,
Toxic love's a cage, and it's our disgrace.

We're caught in the venom, tangled in strife,
An addiction to chaos, slicing through life.
Toxic love's the storm, and it cuts like a knife,
In this deadly dance, we're losing our light.

Inner Demons

In the shadows where the whispers crawl,
    Inner demons scratch, and they're ready to brawl.
    Dark thoughts echo, in the silence they call,
    Fear's a ghostly presence, and it's ready to maul.

Eyes in the mirror, but the soul's not clear,
    Haunted by shadows that only I hear.
    Fighting the ghosts that feed on my fear,
    Inner demons laugh, but they're always near.

Mind's a battlefield, every scar's a wound,
    Demons in the dark, like a cold, dead tune.
    Scratches on my heart, they're a painful monsoon,
    Inner demons dance to a twisted cartoon.

Lost in the maze of my own twisted mind,
    Chains of regret, they're a struggle to find.
    Battles with myself, and I'm left behind,
    Inner demons strike where the light's unkind.

Chasing the nightmares, they're a wicked parade,
    Haunted by the echoes, and the price that I've paid.

Each step through the darkness, where the hopes start to fade,
Inner demons whisper, but the silence's a raid.

Fear's a companion, it's the voice in the dark,
A shadow's a partner, and it's left its mark.
Fighting these phantoms, but they're leaving me stark,
Inner demons reign, and they're tearing apart.

Screams in my head, but they're lost in the roar,
Every corner's a trap, where the shadows implore.
Battles with myself, but the pain's hardcore,
Inner demons thrive, and they're craving for more.

Chains of insecurity, they're a tight, cruel bind,
Locked in the torment, and I'm losing my mind.
Struggling with the fears, but I'm blind to the kind,
Inner demons win, leaving scars undefined.

Shadows in the night, they're a haunting refrain,
Lost in the echoes, and the memories' stain.
Trying to break free, but it's all in vain,
Inner demons dance, and they're driving me insane.

Broken Wings

Fly high, they said, but the sky's out of reach,
Dreams crumbled down, like a lesson to teach.
Wings once strong, now they're frayed at the seam,
Broken promises scatter, like a ghost of a dream.
We soared on ambition, with the world in our grasp,
But the heights we chased are shadows that pass.
Every plan, every hope, like a fading blast,
Broken wings flapping, in the winds of the past.
Cracked dreams, they're a tale of the lost,
Falling from grace, at an endless cost.
Youth's a bright flame, but it's quickly tossed,
Broken wings flutter, but they're feeling the frost.
We were stars in the sky, but the light turned cold,
Dreams shattered like glass, and the tales they told.
The hopes that once soared, now they're stories old,
Broken wings ache, and they're feeling the fold.
Promises made in the heat of the night,
Now they're faded whispers, lost in the fight.
We chased the horizon, but it's out of sight,
Broken wings beating, in the dying light.
Lost in the echoes, where the dreams used to be,
Wings that once flew, now they're dragging, you see.

Every hope that we had, like a ghost in the sea,
Broken wings beating, with a silent plea.
The youth we embraced, now it's fading away,
Promises broken, in the light of the day.
Wings that once carried, now they're frayed and gray,
Broken dreams scatter, like the dust in the fray.
Caught in the wreckage of the dreams we designed,
Falling from grace, with the weight of the bind.
Every shattered hope, like a blade to the mind,
Broken wings falter, leaving shadows behind.
We rise from the ruins, but the scars never fade,
The wings we once had, now they're tattered and frayed.
Broken dreams whisper, in the choices we made,
Broken wings flutter, but they're never remade.

Phoenix Rising

Ash to the wind, where the fire's been burned,
    From the ruins of the past, a lesson is learned.
    Wings of the night, now they're scorched and turned,
    Phoenix rising up, from the embers it's churned.

Cinders in the sky, like the ghost of a flame,
    Broken and battered, but the spirit's untamed.
    From the wreckage we rise, no one's left to blame,
    Phoenix rising higher, through the agony and shame.

Eyes in the smoke, but we're staring at the stars,
    Rising from the ashes, where the battle left scars.
    Every wound, every tear, they're the truth in our bars,
    Phoenix rising strong, with the heat from afar.

Burned to the bone, but we're forging anew,
    From the depths of the dark, there's a light coming through.
    Stronger than before, in the fire we grew,
    Phoenix rising, from the pain we pursue.

Caught in the inferno, but the flames are our guide,
    Through the trials and the storms, we're learning to glide.

Emerging from the darkness, where the shadows collide,
Phoenix rising, with the ashes we ride.

Scars like badges, showing the fight we embraced,
From the ruins of the past, we're finally erased.
Every crack in the shell, it's a tale interlaced,
Phoenix rising, in the heat we're replaced.

We're the spark in the night, igniting the truth,
From the ruins of dreams, and the whispers of youth.
Flying from the fire, in the blaze we find proof,
Phoenix rising, with a roar and a boost.

Soar from the ashes, let the flames be our song,
In the heat of the struggle, we've been tested so long.
From the wreckage we rise, where the broken belong,
Phoenix rising fierce, where the spirits are strong.

Digital Dystopia

Wired up tight, in this digital cage,
   Screens light the night, but they're fueling the rage.
   Eyes on us all, in this twisted stage,
   Digital dystopia, we're trapped in the maze.

Surveillance on blast, every move's on display,
   They're feeding on the data, in a sick, slick way.
   Algorithms rule, while our freedoms decay,
   Digital dystopia, where the mind's led astray.

Clicks and taps, they're the chains on our brain,
   Echoes of control, pulsing through the mainframe.
   We're locked in the code, can't escape the pain,
   Digital dystopia, where they're scripting our shame.

Privacy's dead, it's a ghost in the feed,
   In a world that's wired, they're planting the seed.
   They're watching every step, fulfilling their greed,
   Digital dystopia, where they're pulling the lead.

Eyes on the glass, but the vision's unclear,
   Lost in the static, where they cultivate fear.

They're selling our souls, while we cheer from the rear,
Digital dystopia, where the end's drawing near.

Plugged in deep, we're lost in the stream,
    Reality's a glitch, in this nightmare dream.
    We're puppets on strings, controlled by the scheme,
    Digital dystopia, where they silence the scream.

They sell us a lie, with a smile on the screen,
    A world full of pixels, but the truth's unseen.
    In the matrix of control, we're stuck in between,
    Digital dystopia, where the future's unclean.

Rise up, break out, from this virtual noose,
    We're drowning in code, in the lies they produce.
    In the war of the wires, we've got nothing to lose,
    Digital dystopia, where we fight for the truth.

Unplug the machine, let the real world breathe,
    In the fight for our minds, we're the ones to lead.
    Tear down the walls, where the shadows feed,
    Digital dystopia, where it's time to be freed.

Social Misfit

Born on the edge, where the shadows collide,
Outcast and proud, with nothing to hide.
They try to fit me in, but I slip and slide,
Social misfit, yeah, I live on the wild side.

You want conformity, but I bring the noise,
Breaking all the rules, flipping all the poise.
I'm the glitch in your game, the truth in your ploys,
Social misfit, I'm done being your toy.

They call me strange, say I don't belong,
But I'm writing my own script, singing my own song.
In a world full of right, I'm the beautiful wrong,
Social misfit, where I've been all along.

Tried to cage me in, but I broke the mold,
Refusing to be part of the lies they've sold.
My scars are my armor, my heart's pure gold,
Social misfit, where the truth's uncontrolled.

Don't need your labels, your chains, or your lies,
I see through the mask, see the fear in your eyes.

You try to box me in, but I'll always rise,
Social misfit, where the fire never dies.

I'm the rebel in your ranks, the thorn in your side,
Not living by your rules, not running to hide.
In the land of the fake, I'm the truth that you deride,
Social misfit, wearing difference as my pride.

You can laugh, you can sneer, but I'll never conform,
I'm the eye in your storm, the rage in your norm.
A misfit in your world, but I'm bringing the reform,
Social misfit, in the chaos, I'm the form.

They call me outcast, but I'm free from your chains,
Dancing in the fire, soaking in the rains.
In a world that's insane, I'm the one who remains,
Social misfit, with the courage in my veins.

You can't silence the truth, can't bury the real,
I'm the crack in your walls, the wound you can't heal.
In a world full of masks, I'm the raw, I'm the feel,
Social misfit, where I'm breaking the seal.

So stand tall, all you misfits, all you who defy,
We're the sparks in the dark, the stars in the sky.
In a world full of fake, we're the ones who'll fly,
Social misfit, till the day we die.

Fade to Black

Tick, tick, tick, as the clock unwinds,
  Time slips through, leaving dust behind.
  We chase the sun, but the shadows bind,
  Fade to black, where the truth is blind.

Life's a flash, just a moment in the spin,
  Fighting to hold on, but we can't win.
  Every breath, every step, is wearing thin,
  Fade to black, where it all begins.

We run from the dark, but it's catching fast,
  Holding onto dreams, but they never last.
  We're racing the end, but the die's been cast,
  Fade to black, where the light's outclassed.

Every heartbeat's a step toward the edge,
  Walking the line, on a fragile ledge.
  In the blink of an eye, we're over the hedge,
  Fade to black, where we make our pledge.

We build our walls, thinking they'll stand,
  But the winds of time, they erase the sand.

What's left of us, just slipping through the hand,
Fade to black, where the final strand.

Mortality's a truth that we can't escape,
A shadow on our backs, a form we can't reshape.
We're fading in the dusk, trying to find our shape,
Fade to black, where we all take the scrape.

We're born from the light, but we're drawn to the shade,
Carving our paths, in the hopes that they don't fade.
But the end is a certainty, the last card played,
Fade to black, where the debts are paid.

Whispers in the dark, echoes in the mind,
Searching for meaning, but it's hard to find.
In the end, we're just another name, unsigned,
Fade to black, where the soul's unkind.

So we fight, we rage, against the dying light,
Holding onto moments, with all our might.
But the night comes quick, swallowing the sight,
Fade to black, where we end the fight.

In the end, we all face the same track,
No matter the journey, no turning back.
We're all just shadows, on the same old rack,
Fade to black, where the world goes slack.

Urban Exodus

Concrete jungle, where the echoes clash,
   City lights blind, turning dreams to ash.
   Caught in the grind, where the shadows thrash,
   Urban exodus, where we break from the crash.

Skyscrapers rise, but the soul sinks low,
   In the maze of steel, where the cold winds blow.
   Chasing paper trails, but there's nothing to show,
   Urban exodus, where the rivers flow.

Noise on blast, drowning out the mind,
   Lost in the crowd, where the lost ones find.
   Searching for peace, but it's hard to unwind,
   Urban exodus, where the chains unbind.

Streetlights flicker, but the darkness grows,
   In the heart of the city, where nobody knows.
   Looking for escape, where the wild wind blows,
   Urban exodus, where the green grass grows.

City life pulls, but it's wearing thin,
   In the hustle and the bustle, where do we begin?

Running from the smog, where the air feels thin,
Urban exodus, where the woods let us in.

Skid marks fade, as we leave behind,
    The noise, the smoke, where the gears grind.
    In the arms of nature, we're no longer blind,
    Urban exodus, where the stars align.

Steel and glass, they crumble to rust,
    In the shadow of the trees, where we place our trust.
    Leaving behind the city's lust,
    Urban exodus, where the earth's a must.

Footsteps echo on a path unknown,
    Where the city's grip is overthrown.
    Finding peace where the seeds are sown,
    Urban exodus, where we're finally home.

Escape the grind, leave the noise behind,
    Find a place where the air's unconfined.
    In the arms of nature, we unwind,
    Urban exodus, where the soul's redesigned.

The Price of Fame

Lights on blast, but the shadows are deep,
    Fame's a drug that won't let you sleep.
    Chasing the highs, but the lows cut steep,
    The price of fame, where the wolves all creep.

Flashing lights, but the darkness remains,
    Cameras click, but they're capturing pains.
    You're the headline, but you're losing your reins,
    The price of fame, where the soul's in chains.

Everyone's watching, but nobody sees,
    You're trapped in a glass house, down on your knees.
    They build you up just to watch you freeze,
    The price of fame, where freedom's a tease.

They want your image, but not the truth,
    Chasing your ghost, but they steal your youth.
    Every move's a trap, every word's a sleuth,
    The price of fame, where lies take root.

Privacy's gone, just a relic of the past,
    They feed on your pain, but the feast won't last.

You're drowning in the gold, but sinking fast,
The price of fame, where your life's outcast.

Whispers in the dark, but the silence screams,
Trapped in the glare of the broken dreams.
You're a puppet on strings, torn at the seams,
The price of fame, where nothing's as it seems.

You sold your name for a place in the light,
But the cost was your soul, now nothing feels right.
You're losing the fight in the dead of the night,
The price of fame, where the stars burn bright.

They cheer your name, but it's hollow and cold,
You're just another story, a tale to be told.
Fame's a dealer, and your life's been sold,
The price of fame, where the glitter's turned old.

The pressure mounts, and the cracks begin to show,
You're standing tall, but the ground's below.
The world's at your feet, but you've nowhere to go,
The price of fame, where the spotlight's a foe.

In the end, you're left with the shadows you made,
The light fades out, and the memories cascade.
You paid the price, but the debt's been delayed,
The price of fame, where the soul's betrayed.

Battle Scars

These scars on my skin, they run deep as the night,
    Memories etched in a constant fight.
    Every wound, every cut, is a story in spite,
    Battle scars, where the pain ignites.

Fists clenched tight, but the mind's gone numb,
    Living in the echoes where the nightmares drum.
    You can see the marks, but the feelings are dumb,
    Battle scars, where the silence hums.

They say I'm a survivor, but the cost is steep,
    Haunted by the shadows that never sleep.
    Tears I can't cry, but the hurt's buried deep,
    Battle scars, where the heart starts to seep.

Each day's a war, with no end in sight,
    The battle's internal, but it's clear in the light.
    You see me standing, but I'm losing the fight,
    Battle scars, where the darkness bites.

Blood stains fade, but the soul won't heal,
    Carrying the weight of the blade and the steel.

They don't see the damage, but the pain's real,
Battle scars, where the truth reveals.

It's not just the skin, it's the mind torn apart,
Wounds that don't show, but they live in the heart.
You fight to stay whole, but you're breaking apart,
Battle scars, where the nightmares start.

The world moves on, but you're stuck in the past,
Running from the shadows that never cast.
You're wearing a mask, but it's fading fast,
Battle scars, where the die's been cast.

Ink on the skin, but the hurt's in the bone,
You fight through the crowds, but you're always alone.
They don't hear the screams in the monotone,
Battle scars, where the pain's overgrown.

Each breath's a reminder of the war you've survived,
But the peace that you seek, it's been deprived.
You're alive in the flesh, but the soul's been knived,
Battle scars, where the pain's revived.

So here I stand, with my armor worn thin,
In a war with myself, that I'll never win.
Every mark is a battle, but the war's within,
Battle scars, where the end begins.

Lost Generation

We're the lost ones, drifting in the dark,
  Searching for a flame, but we can't find a spark.
  Trapped in a cycle where the silence barks,
  Lost generation, where the futures arc.

Screens lit up, but the soul's gone black,
  Chasing dreams in a world off-track.
  The noise surrounds, but the echoes lack,
  Lost generation, where we can't turn back.

We're plugged in, but we're tuning out,
  Voices in our heads, filled with doubt.
  The truth's a whisper, drowned by the shout,
  Lost generation, where the fires go out.

They sold us lies wrapped in gold and gloss,
  Told us we're winners, but they rigged the toss.
  Now we're left picking up the cost,
  Lost generation, where the lines are crossed.

We're the ones who were born to stray,
  Searching for meaning in the disarray.

But the more we search, the more we fray,
Lost generation, where we fade away.

They built a world on the bones of the past,
Told us it's the future, but it's fading fast.
Now we're left to carry the cast,
Lost generation, where the die's been cast.

We're the voices that scream but never heard,
Drowning in a sea of every empty word.
The world spins on, but it's all absurd,
Lost generation, where the lines are blurred.

They promised hope, but delivered despair,
Left us to choke on the toxic air.
Now we're gasping, but they don't care,
Lost generation, where the truth's laid bare.

We're the ashes of a flame burned bright,
Trying to find our way in the endless night.
But the road's gone cold, there's no end in sight,
Lost generation, where we fight for the light.

So here we stand, with our backs to the wall,
Waiting for the day when we don't fall.
But the ground's unsteady, and the stakes are tall,
Lost generation, where we answer the call.

The Outsider's Perspective

I'm the outsider, peering through the cracks,
   Watching society crumble, losing track.
   Your norms are chains, but they never lack,
   The outsider's perspective, where the truth attacks.

You parade your masks, but the smiles are thin,
   Living in the system, but it's all a spin.
   I see the facade where the darkness begins,
   The outsider's perspective, where the honesty wins.

You're trapped in your bubbles, floating high and clear,
   But I'm down in the grime, where the truth is near.
   You claim you're free, but it's all insincere,
   The outsider's perspective, where the lies disappear.

You chase the glitter, while the streets are cracked,
   Trading your soul for a golden pact.
   I see through the gloss, while the world's been hacked,
   The outsider's perspective, where the shadows act.

Your voices are loud, but they're hollow inside,
   Screaming for change, but you're lost in the ride.

I watch as the system keeps you tied,
The outsider's perspective, where the truth won't hide.

You build your towers on the backs of the weak,
Climbing to the top, but the foundation's meek.
I see the cracks in your world, so bleak,
The outsider's perspective, where the lies speak.

You're blind to the cracks in your own glass dome,
Living in comfort while the others roam.
I see the emptiness beneath your chrome,
The outsider's perspective, where the truth's overthrown.

You sell your ideals, but the worth is false,
Claiming you're free while you dance on the pulse.
I'm down here, seeing the world's convulse,
The outsider's perspective, where the facade's a waltz.

You spin your tales while the chaos grows,
Painting your world in a filtered pose.
I see the wreckage where the truth's exposed,
The outsider's perspective, where the mask deposes.

You think you're safe in your bubble of light,
But I'm out in the dark, seeing the plight.
You're trapped in the day, but I'm awake at night,
The outsider's perspective, where the flaws ignite.

So keep your illusions, I'm fine where I stand,
Watching the chaos, understanding the land.
Your truth is a script, but I see the brand,

The outsider's perspective, where the truth's unplanned.

Unwritten Rules

Welcome to the grind where the shadows rule,
  The streets have codes, they don't teach in school.
  Unwritten rules, but they're sharp as a tool,
  Life's a tightrope, and we're breaking the cool.

You walk these streets, gotta keep your head low,
  Respect's a currency, and the debts always grow.
  Play your cards right, but the deck's a shadow show,
  Unwritten rules, where the truth's a blow.

Every block's got a rhythm, a beat, a rhyme,
  You step out of line, and you're doing time.
  In the alley's silence, the danger climbs,
  Unwritten rules, where the sins prime.

Eyes in the dark, they're watching your back,
  One wrong move, and they'll keep you off track.
  It's a game of survival, no room to slack,
  Unwritten rules, where the shadows attack.

You're born in the mix, where the whispers hide,
  The street's got a language, no truth to confide.

You follow the code, or you get pushed aside,
Unwritten rules, where the darks collide.

Every gesture's a signal, every glance a cue,
The lines are blurred, but you know what to do.
You play the game, or you pay the due,
Unwritten rules, where the stakes accrue.

Trust is a ghost in the land of the lost,
In the jungle of the streets, it's a heavy cost.
You learn fast, or you're forever tossed,
Unwritten rules, where the lines are crossed.

They don't write it down, but you feel the weight,
In every silent moment, you seal your fate.
You're part of the system, whether it's love or hate,
Unwritten rules, where the ghosts await.

In the cracks of the pavement, the codes are scribed,
In the echoes of the night, the lessons are bribed.
You live by the whispers, or you'll be deprived,
Unwritten rules, where the truth's contrived.

So walk the line, with your eyes open wide,
In the world of shadows, there's no place to hide.
You follow the code, or you're cast aside,
Unwritten rules, where the darkness guides.

Echoes of the Underground

We're the echoes of a world that's torn,
Roaming through the chaos, where the rules are worn.
The underground hums with a vibe forlorn,
Where the lost souls meet and the dreams are scorned.

Concrete jungles where the shadows play,
We're the noise in the silence, where the truth frays.
Walking the tightrope, in the harshest way,
Echoes of the underground, where the ghosts sway.

Chains on our ankles, but our minds are free,
The system's a cage, but we're the decree.
We speak in the whispers, in the darkened spree,
Echoes of the underground, where we find the key.

The lights are dim, and the streets are cracked,
Voices are hushed, but the whispers pack.
Every corner hides a story, a silent attack,
Echoes of the underground, where the pain's stacked.

In the grime and the grit, we forge our path,
Where the pressure builds up, and the fury's wrath.

The shadows are our comrades, in this aftermath,
Echoes of the underground, where the truth's a blast.

We're the remnants of a system that's failed,
In the darkened alleys, where the rebels prevailed.
Every shout's a scream, every silence hailed,
Echoes of the underground, where the spirit's unveiled.

Life's a battle, and the scars are deep,
We fight for the voice that the silence keeps.
In the realm of the forgotten, where the night seeps,
Echoes of the underground, where the spirit leaps.

We're the fire in the night, the spark in the void,
In a world that's broken, where hope's destroyed.
Our echoes rise up, never to be toyed,
Echoes of the underground, where the rebels are buoyed.

So hear the call in the hollow and the raw,
We're the heartbeat of a world with flaws.
We rise in the silence, defying the laws,
Echoes of the underground, where the spirit draws.

Broken Systems

Welcome to the edge where the system cracks,
   We're the rebels in the shadows, pushing back.
   Broken systems, where the truth attacks,
   Caught in the gears, feeling the cracks.

The machine's got gears that grind and seize,
   Promises sold with no chance to appease.
   We're the voices lost in the deafening breeze,
   Broken systems, where the noise won't ease.

See the chains in the cold, harsh light,
   Each link's a story of the endless fight.
   We're the sparks in the dark, igniting the night,
   Broken systems, where the wrong feels right.

They sell us dreams on a silver screen,
   But the reality's harsh, and the truth's unseen.
   We're the echoes of a world so mean,
   Broken systems, where the light's not clean.

In the cracks of the concrete, we find our way,
   Treading through the lies, day after day.

We're the fire that burns in the endless gray,
Broken systems, where we never sway.

The power's a facade, built on broken trust,
The promises fade and turn to dust.
We're the rebels in the system, never adjusted,
Broken systems, where the truth's combusted.

Every crack in the wall is a voice in the dark,
Every broken piece is a sign of the spark.
We rise from the ruins, we leave our mark,
Broken systems, where the truth's stark.

So we shout from the rubble, from the heart of the fight,
In the echoes of the chaos, we find our might.
We're the remnants of a world that's not quite right,
Broken systems, where the shadows ignite.

Concrete Shadows

Welcome to the grid where the darkness breathes,
Where the walls whisper lies through the steel-wrought
sheaves.
Concrete shadows stretch and weave,
In the silence, truth deceives.

Neon lights flicker like a dying pulse,
In the city's heart, every dream is dulled.
We're the ghosts in the grid, the tales are scrolled,
Concrete shadows, where the truth's been sold.

Walk the cracks of a world that's cold and stark,
Where hope's a spark in a sea of dark.
We fight with shadows, leave a mark,
Concrete shadows, where the rage embarks.

In the alleys of noise, where the echoes scream,
We're the rebels who burn with a furious gleam.
Shattered illusions, not what they seem,
Concrete shadows, where we chase the dream.

The streets are a battlefield, the war's unkind,

We're the lost souls in the grind.
Every step's a fight, every breath's confined,
Concrete shadows, where the truth's blind.

We're the whispers in the rubble, the cries in the void,
In the land of the forgotten, we're the paranoid.
Every lie's a shackle, every promise a ploy,
Concrete shadows, where the dreams are destroyed.

The city's a beast with a metal jaw,
It chews up the spirit, leaves it raw.
We're the rebels in the night, breaking the law,
Concrete shadows, where the system's flawed.

Rise from the ashes, we ignite the blaze,
In the darkest corners, we'll set our ways.
We're the fire in the storm, the light in the haze,
Concrete shadows, where the truth's ablaze.

So keep your eyes open, don't fall for the trap,
In the silence of the city, hear the snap.
We're the heartbeat of the dark, the world's gap,
Concrete shadows, where the shadows clap.

Razor's Edge

We're dancing on the razor's edge, where the lines blur,
   In a world that's cold, every promise a slur.
   Treading the chaos, where the shadows stir,
   Razor's edge, where the truths defer.

The city's pulse beats with a hollow sound,
   We're the whispers in the noise, where the lost are found.
   Each step's a risk, each move's profound,
   Razor's edge, where the dreams are drowned.

We're the sparks in the dark, igniting the flame,
   In a world of false glory, where the shadows claim.
   We're the echoes of rage, never the same,
   Razor's edge, where we're breaking the chain.

The system's a trap with a silver face,
   Promises sold in a high-stakes race.
   We're the rebels on the edge, in a wild chase,
   Razor's edge, where we find our place.

Eyes wide open in a world that's blind,
   Every truth's twisted, every path's confined.

We're the fire in the void, the clarity we find,
Razor's edge, where the bold unwind.

In the cracks of the pavement, the truth's concealed,
We're the voices of the lost, the dreams revealed.
The edge is sharp, but our spirit's healed,
Razor's edge, where the darkness is sealed.

We're the pulse in the silence, the break in the norm,
In a world that's shattered, we rise from the storm.
We're the heat in the night, the rebel's form,
Razor's edge, where the spirit's born.

So we walk this line, with a fire in our eyes,
In the realm of shadows, where the falsehoods lie.
We're the rebels in the dark, reaching for the sky,
Razor's edge, where the truth won't die.

Broken Chains

Welcome to the streets where the echoes scream,
We're the lost souls chasing a fractured dream.
Broken chains rattle in the night's dark gleam,
In a world of shadows, nothing's as it seems.

The city's a cage with a polished facade,
Every hope's a gamble, every truth's flawed.
We're the sparks in the void, the rebels applaud,
Broken chains, where the silence is flawed.

We fight in the alleys where the darkness thrives,
Every breath's a struggle, every moment survives.
We're the whispers of rage in the deadened lives,
Broken chains, where the spirit revives.

The system's a puppet with strings of deceit,
We're the fire in the storm, the heart's fierce beat.
In the chaos and noise, we rise to defeat,
Broken chains, where the rebels meet.

The lies are a trap with a glittering sheen,
Every truth is buried where the shadows convene.

We're the rebels on the edge, the untamed scene,
Broken chains, where the nightmares convene.

Walk the line of fury with the darkness in tow,
Every step's a battle, every word's a blow.
We're the voices of truth in a world of woe,
Broken chains, where the raw winds blow.

We carve out the path in the shattered remains,
In a land of illusions, where the falsehoods reign.
We're the pulse of defiance, the fire in the veins,
Broken chains, where the pain sustains.

So let the chains fall, let the rebellion ignite,
In the heart of the chaos, we'll claim our right.
We're the rebels in the storm, the beacon of light,
Broken chains, where the truth takes flight.